Dear Parents,

Welcome to the Scholastic Reader series. We have taken over 80 years of experience with teachers, parents, and children and put it into a program that is designed to match your child's interests and skills.

Level 1—Short sentences and stories made up of words kids can sound out using their phonics skills and words that are important to remember.

Level 2—Longer sentences and stories with words kids need to know and new "big" words that they will want to know.

Level 3—From sentences to paragraphs to longer stories, these books have large "chunks" of texts and are made up of a rich vocabulary.

Level 4—First chapter books with more words and fewer pictures.

It is important that children learn to read well enough to succeed in school and beyond. Here are ideas for reading this book with your child:

- Look at the book together. Encourage your child to read the title and make a prediction about the story.
- Read the book together. Encourage your child to sound out words when appropriate. When your child struggles, you can help by providing the word.
- Encourage your child to retell the story. This is a great way to check for comprehension.
- Have your child take the fluency test on the last page to check progress.

Scholastic Readers are designed to support your child's efforts to learn how to read at every age and every stage. Enjoy helping your child learn to read and love to read.

      —Francie Alexander
        Chief Education Officer
        Scholastic Education

Text and illustrations copyright © 2006 by Jacqueline Rogers.
Activities copyright © 2006 by Scholastic Inc.

Library of Congress Cataloging-in-Publication Data available

ISBN: 0-439-72501-1

10 9 8 7 6 5 4 3 2 1   5 6 7 8 9 10/0

Printed in the U.S.A. 23 • First printing, October 2005

Goose on the Loose

**Written and Illustrated by
Jacqueline Rogers**

Scholastic Reader — Level 1

Cartwheel
·B·O·O·K·S·®

SCHOLASTIC INC.
New York   Toronto   London   Auckland   Sydney
Mexico City   New Delhi   Hong Kong   Buenos Aires

It is almost playtime.

Jen and I pick up scraps.

Liz puts the scissors away.

Millie puts the glue
sticks away.

Ted puts the
markers away.

Playtime is here!
We line up. I am first.

"Don't run,"
says Mrs. Miller.

John and I play with a big yellow ball.

"Look," says John.
"I see a goose."

The goose honks.

"Look," I say. "I see
a baby goose."

The baby goose
is alone.

I want to help it find
its mother.

"STOP!" says
Mrs. Miller.
"The geese
are afraid of us.
We must be
very still."

We try to be
very still.

But John
drops the
ball.

And Henry
sniffs.

Jenna coughs.

Mrs. Miller whispers, "We must be very, very quiet."

The mother
goose honks.
The baby starts
to run to her.

But Rachel sneezes.

The baby runs away.

We are all still again.
The mother goose
honks again.
And the baby starts
to run to her.

This time, I hiccup.
The baby runs away again!

At last, we are still, still, still.

The baby runs to the mother.

The mother and baby
are together at last.
We are so happy.

In our classroom,
we draw pictures
of the happy geese.